If I Could Ride a Train

If I Could
Ride a Train

Written and Illustrated by

Heidi Koland

NEW YORK

LONDON • NASHVILLE • MELBOURNE • VANCOUVER

If I Could Ride a Train

Published in New York, New York, by Morgan James Publishing. Morgan James is a trademark of Morgan James, LLC. www.MorganJamesPublishing.com

Proudly distributed by Ingram Publisher Services.

Morgan James BOGO™

A **FREE** ebook edition is available for you or a friend with the purchase of this print book.

CLEARLY SIGN YOUR NAME ABOVE

Instructions to claim your free ebook edition:
1. Visit MorganJamesBOGO.com
2. Sign your name CLEARLY in the space above
3. Complete the form and submit a photo of this entire page
4. You or your friend can download the ebook to your preferred device

ISBN 9781631957376 paperback
ISBN 9781631958250 case laminate
ISBN 9781631957383 ebook
Library of Congress Control Number: 2021945130

Cover and Interior Design by:
Chris Treccani
www.3dogcreative.net

Morgan James PUBLISHING **Builds** with... **Habitat for Humanity** Peninsula and Greater Williamsburg

Morgan James is a proud partner of Habitat for Humanity Peninsula and Greater Williamsburg. Partners in building since 2006.

Get involved today! Visit MorganJamesPublishing.com/giving-back

This book belongs to:

_____

All Aboard!

If I could ride a train today,
I would smile so big with glee!
I'd hop aboard when the conductor called
and sit beside my family.

The big engine would roar and chug,
two toots to say, " Let's go! "
I'd sit and watch the world go by,
enjoying the dazzling show.

We'd zip past stations and glide over hills,
climb steep mountain passes too.
Whisk into big, dark tunnels and
out the other side ... breakthrough!

Into the glorious morning sun,
the canyon by my side,
we'd chug along, my family and me,
Enjoying the beautiful ride.

Dash across rugged mountain trestles,
spanning rivers oh-so-wide,
watching the gurgling, rocky water
carve through the stones and glide . . .

down through the canyon and beyond;
I'd imagine where the water must go.
Through the plains and to the sea,
moving fast at first, then slow.

We'd leave the river dream behind
and keep going on our way.
I'd count the cars to pass the time;
It's a game I like to play.

I love to explore the world by train,
especially the diesel kind.
We'd all sit together and look outside,
talking about the cool things, which we'd find.

A passenger car is where we'd ride.
It feels so incredibly free.
It's a way for people to explore the world
and see everything there is to see!

We'd have had such fun on the train today,
exploring so many wonderful things.
The train would begin to creak and slow,
and the whistle would begin to sing.

We'd rumble back home to the station,

one toot to say we're through.

Time to step off our railroad journey.

" Goodbye train! I had so much fun with you! "

About the Author

Heidi Koland is infinitely curious about the world around her. She spent her childhood exploring the outdoors - camping, hiking, and, later, photographing her experiences; she has extended that curiosity into appreciation of the natural beauty surrounding us daily.

A free ebook edition is available with the purchase of this book.

To claim your free ebook edition:

1. Visit MorganJamesBOGO.com
2. Sign your name CLEARLY in the space
3. Complete the form and submit a photo of the entire copyright page
4. You or your friend can download the ebook to your preferred device

Morgan James BOGO™

A **FREE** ebook edition is available for you or a friend with the purchase of this print book.

CLEARLY SIGN YOUR NAME ABOVE

Instructions to claim your free ebook edition:
1. Visit MorganJamesBOGO.com
2. Sign your name CLEARLY in the space above
3. Complete the form and submit a photo of this entire page
4. You or your friend can download the ebook to your preferred device

Print & Digital Together Forever.

Snap a photo

Free ebook

Read anywhere